MW01132947

Table of Contents

About the Author – page 5

Introduction – page 8

Chapter One "The Fight Begins in the Womb" – page 10

Chapter Two "The Daily Fights of Spina Bifida" – page 14

Chapter Three "Struggles of Surgeries and Hospital Stays" – page 18

Chapter Four "What is a Shunt" – page 27

Chapter Five "Living with Incontinence" – page 31

1

Chapter Six "A Mix of Medications" – page 35

Chapter Seven "Gaining Control and Being Discreet" – page 39

Chapter Eight "The Struggle with Mobility" – page 43

Chapter Nine "Keeping a Balanced Diet and Weight" – page 48

Chapter Ten "Living with Allergies" – page 53

Chapter Eleven "Having Confidence and a Positive Attitude" – page 58

Chapter Twelve "Having Family Support" – page - 62

Chapter Thirteen "Life Altering Modifications" – page 68

Chapter Fourteen "Facing the World" – page 73

Chapter Fifteen "Being Accepted: Fitting In" – page 81

Chapter Sixteen "School with a Disability" page - 88

Chapter Seventeen "The Ability to Be Involved in Activities" – page 93

Chapter Eighteen "Learning How to Drive" – page 102

Chapter Nineteen "Entering Adulthood with a Disability" – page 107

Chapter Twenty "The Struggles of College and Finding a Job" – page 111

Chapter Twenty One "Healthy Relationships in Love" – page 115

Chapter Twenty Two "Starting a Family" – page 119

Acknowledgements – page 123

The Life of a Spina Bifida Warrior

By: Amanda Fatula

About the Author

My name is Amanda and I am a Spina Bifida warrior. I have lived with the disability for 31 years and have overcome many things that many did not think were possible. I have a fulltime job, a loving family that I still live with and amazing friends who understand and accept me for who I am. My life has not been easy but I have pushed through the struggle and accomplished many things. I may not be able to do everything I would like to do but I try doing them to the best of my ability.

Every year from the time I was 10 years old I have attended some kind of camp for children and/or adults with the same disability as me. The best part is being around people who understand me and know exactly what I'm

5

going through. Staying with friends has taught me that teamwork is sometimes the key to getting things done that I normally could not do on my own. I'm always telling my family things that I've done with my friends and they are amazed at what I can accomplish. Not because they don't think I'm capable but because they're so used to helping me with things that sometimes they don't realize what I am actually capable of.

I am working full time as a secretary in the laboratory of our local hospital. I have been there since November 2011. I have learned many skills and have grown a lot since working with my coworkers. They have learned how to best help me and I have also learned when to ask for help. I don't always like to ask, I like to do things on my own. I am used to being independent and not having to rely so much on anyone but I'm slowly learning that sometimes it just isn't possible or safe. My coworkers are very good about doing things for me that I can't do myself.

Over the years things have changed for me and I'm no longer able to do what I used to but I have made changes to my life to be able to get things done. My family has been very supportive when it comes to making adaptations and changes for me. We have gotten work done to our home to make it more accessible and have come to terms with the fact that things are changing. Accepting the change was the hardest part of the whole thing for all of us. I never liked to admit I needed help or things were difficult but I've learned in order to move forward with my life I need to accept things for how they are and make necessary changes to move on.

My hope for this book is to teach people a little bit about Spina Bifida. I would like to show them that just because someone has a disability doesn't mean they can't survive in a world just like everyone else. Just because someone may have to do things a little differently they are still a person just like everyone else! With love and support they're able to conquer anything!

Introduction

      The life of an individual with Spina Bifida is never an easy one. There are many surgeries involved and often mobility restrictions. Problems with sensation and incontinence could also be some things an individual will have to deal with. Children and adults with Spina Bifida can and often do lead normal lives with the help of adaptations, family, friends and organizations. Some adaptations may include modifications to homes and cars or maybe just doing things a little differently. No matter how an individual with Spina Bifida gets things in everyday life accomplished the main thing is they did it! Most individuals are reluctant to ask for help because they are ashamed or feel like they are a burden to others. They often make their own ways of doing things just to get it done on their own without help. The motto for most Spina Bifida individuals is "It may not always be the RIGHT way but it's MY way."

My hope for this is to educate people about Spina Bifida. As well as giving them a different view of individuals with this disability. Just because someone looks or does things differently than someone else does not mean the person is weird or strange. It just means they do not have the same abilities as others and that's okay. Hopefully, this will also teach people ways to help an individual with a disability without being offensive. Often time's people have the right intention to help someone but, the way they handle the situation may not always be the best. Being helpful but also taking into consideration that just because it may not seem like the right way to accomplish something to someone, it just may be the right way for someone else.

Chapter One

"The Fight Begins in the Womb"

An infant born with Spina Bifida, also called "split spine", has a fight that begins in the womb. An ultrasound that is performed during the mother's routine checkups will determine if the child does indeed have Spina Bifida. The mother can also have an alpha-feto-protein (AFP) blood test done around the 16th week of pregnancy. A high AFP can mean that the baby does have Spina Bifida. She has to make sure to stay as healthy as possible, taking the proper vitamins and medications during pregnancy. Spina Bifida is not something that can be prevented and is never anyone's fault but making sure to take folic acid and other vitamins could help minimize the chances of it occurring. It has been said that one of the things that can increase the chances of having Spina Bifida is having of a folic acid deficiency.

There are 4 different forms of Spina Bifida. The most severe form is Myelomeningocele. Several symptoms include: an open spinal canal over some vertebrae, usually in the middle or lower part of the back. The membranes and the spinal cord could be pushed outside of the back in an exposed or skin covered sac. This can result in weak or paralyzed leg muscles, seizures, deformed feet, hips that are uneven, a curved spine known as scoliosis, some bowel and/or bladder complications. Hydrocephalus could also be present; this is a buildup of fluid in the brain.

Meningocele is another form of Spina Bifida where a small moist sac or cyst protrudes through the gap in the spine. The sac contains a portion of the spinal cord membrane or meninges and spinal fluid. The sac may be covered with skin or part of the spinal cord membrane. It will contain little or no nerve tissue.

The third form of Spina Bifida is Occulta, which actually means "hidden". In this case there is a gap between the vertebrae, no visible opening outside, and no fluid-filled sac outside the body. A small birthmark or dimple appears on the back at the location of paralysis, there is a small group or cluster of hair on the back. There is also an area of extra fat on the back. A person with Spina Bifida Occulta may not even know they have this condition. It is the less severe; little to no defects. It is also the most common form.

Closed neural tube defects make up the 4th form of Spina Bifida. It consists of a diverse group of defects in which the spinal cord is marked by malformations of fat, bone or meninges. In most instances there are few or no symptoms; in others the malformation causes incomplete paralysis with urinary and bowel dysfunctions.

Today there are many things that can be done to help prevent or lessen the chance of an infant being paralyzed at birth. An operation can be done to the mother and infant while the child is still in utero. In this procedure, the infant is removed from the mother's womb, surgery is performed to close the opening on the back and the infant is placed back in the womb for the remainder of the pregnancy. There have been many success stories related to this surgery. Children can be born with little to no abnormalities at all. Spina Bifida is a complex condition that varies from one person to another. Just because you see one person who can do certain things does not mean it's the same for others.

Chapter Two

"The Daily Fights of Spina Bifida"

The daily routines of Spina Bifida individuals start first thing in the morning. The simple task of getting out of bed can be difficult for some. Many need extra assistance when dressing, transferring, and doing morning rituals. There are bathroom problems that may need to be taken care of which includes self-catheterizing, and bowel regimens.

Sometimes when a child is younger they need to wear a back brace to keep their back and legs straight while they sleep. When I was younger I would have to wear what was called a "mummy wrap" that went from under my arms to my ankles to keep my body straight. This was to try to correct the curvature of my back and the stiffness of the tendons in my knees. It was very uncomfortable and I did not like having to wear it but it did help in the long run. Some individuals need assistance when getting in and out of the shower. Even feeding or cooking for themselves can become a struggle. There are some individuals that are more independent and able to do these things on their own but it's always not that simple for many. These tasks can be tiresome, because it takes a lot more energy for someone with a disability to get a shower, get dressed and even move than most people.

When I was a child getting up and out of bed wasn't much of a problem for me. I had the mobility to do what needed to be done to get started for my day. I was able to get in and out of bed by myself and even dress or shower. The hardest thing for me was not being able to reach things. Some things were just too high because I was always so small. I would have to find other ways to get what I wanted whether it was asking for help or climbing up on something to be just a little higher. My family never liked when I tried climbing to reach things because of how dangerous it was. I have learned to do things safely but sometimes it still requires climbing.

From the time I was little steps were always a fight. I could go up and down easier without my braces because I could either crawl or scoot backwards on my behind. As I got older using my crutches and braces to navigate the stairs has become harder. There are many things I can't do on my own. My shoulders and arms don't have the strength that they used to, I have also lost strength in my legs making it harder to get where I need to go.

If there are no railings there is no chance of me being able to do stairs by myself. Someone would either have to help me or physically pick me up in order to get to where I'm trying to go. It's very frustrating because I try to be as independent as I can but I feel like I'm not because I always have to ask for help. If I'm in my own house I'm able to scoot up and down the stairs on my behind with no problem. If I'm out at someone else's house, it's a little embarrassing to do this. Sometimes doing that could even be a problem if the stairs are high or narrow. If there is a railing that I'm able to support myself on then I could navigate the stairs if I had to.

Every day is always a struggle for us but we do what we can to push through. My Spina Bifida friends and others I've seen are some of the strongest people I've ever met. The courage we have, and the strength to push through everything we are faced with is just amazing to me. There are days I wonder how much more I can handle but I think to myself "if I don't do this, what kind of example am I setting for others in my position?" I have to keep going!

Chapter Three

"Struggles of Surgeries and Hospital Stays"

Over the first few days of life an infant with Spina Bifida will have to endure being poked and prodded as well as various surgeries. It is not uncommon for individuals with a disability to require many surgeries throughout their lives. Some can have up to 50 or more during an entire lifetime. Many may spend the majority of their childhood in and out of hospitals due to surgeries. This is because as a child grows the bones and muscles are changing so adjustments need to be made to correct any issues that may arise later on.

Some surgeries include the placement of a shunt. The reason for needing this is because most Spina Bifida patients' bodies do not drain cerebrospinal fluid (CSF) on its own. Fluid buildup is called hydrocephalus and can cause many problems if not taken care of early enough. Some symptoms of needing a shunt or a replacement in an infant are swelling of the head and vomiting. Later in life as a child gets older the symptoms can change to headaches, blurred vision and being dizzy. As a child gets older they will be able to better communicate with their parents what's going on or how they're feeling.

Another major surgery that is common after birth is the closure of the back. This is to prevent infection and further damage to the nerves and spinal cord. Depending on the location of the opening will determine the amount of sensation and mobility the child will have as they start to walk and become more mobile. As the child grows sometimes the spine will try attaching itself to other tissue known as "tethering." When this happens the child will need to have surgery to detach the spine from the scar tissue. This is a complicated surgery due to the fact that it can cause the child to lose more mobility, sensation and pain. Other back surgeries that may be required as a child are to treat scoliosis, which is a sideways curvature of the spine in an "S" shape, and kyphosis, a spine that bends forward or hunchback."

Many infants will spend the first 2-3 months in the hospital due to having surgeries and having to be monitored for any other problems that may arise. Some children will need reconstructive surgery on their bowels and bladder later in life due to lack of sensation and control. Most children with Spina Bifida will require help going to the bathroom. A large portion of individuals will need to self-catheterize them self to empty their bladder. This is because of weak muscles; they are unable to empty their bladder on their own. As children get older they often need surgery to correct bowel problems as well. One surgery that can be done is called the ACE procedure.

Most children will need to have surgery on their legs, hips and feet. This is because the muscles are weaker than others and tighter due to the fact that the child is most likely spending most of their time sitting. Knee and hip releases are common, this is where they take the tendons in the knees and hips and loosen them to give the child more flexibility. Sometimes surgery is needed on their feet because the feet turn sideways when they shouldn't called clubfoot. For any of these surgeries the child will need to be casted for up to 4-6 weeks. During this time it can become even more difficult and sometimes even impossible for the individual to move around as normal without assistance.

Casting can make transfers difficult because of being unable to bend the same way as before. I know I needed extra help during this time. While casted for those who can feel the affected area it can become very itchy. Being creative in ways to get the itch to go away is something many learn quickly. Whether it's a ruler, pen or anything long and skinny the individual will do whatever it takes to make that itch go away.

These are just a few of the many surgeries an individual with Spina Bifida will have to endure. Some also need shunt revisions because of blocked or detached tubing. There are other reasons to have a shunt revision as well, such as the device just stops functioning.

After I was born I was taken into surgery for the closure of my back. My spine was exposed causing me to be paralyzed from the waist down. I have always had to wear a larger brace on my left leg to my upper thigh because I have no muscle strength in that leg. I am not able to move my left leg at all and have no feeling in it. On my right leg I just wear a smaller brace to support my ankle. My right leg was the stronger of the two when I was younger but as I got older I did lose function in that leg as well because of having multiple back surgeries.

In junior high I had surgery for "tethered cord." After surgery I started to have a lot of problems with bowel control. I had no feeling of when I had to go as well as no control to hold it. Going into high school I didn't want to deal with that so I talked to my doctor about what I could do. That's when he suggested the ACE procedure. It was one of the toughest surgeries I had ever done but in my opinion the most rewarding. I didn't have to worry about having accidents anymore and I finally felt like I had my life back.

The summer before I was entering high school I had the ACE procedure done, where they connect the intestines to the appendix and bring it to either the side or belly button. They had to use my belly button because my appendix was too short to bring to the side. I had a 6 inch incision going down the middle of my stomach, and catheter in my belly button for 6 weeks until everything was healed enough to take it out. This made it hard to move because I was afraid of pulling the catheter out. I had to make sure I kept the incision clean before and even after doing the ACE treatment. Doctors have told me that the process of doing my ACE should only take about 30-45 minutes in the bathroom but it takes me sometimes up to 2 hours. We have never been able to figure out what causes this big time difference for me. It's just something I've had to learn to deal with.

To do the process for the ACE I have to insert a catheter in my belly button and flush with 500-1000 ml of warm soapy water. The soap I use is the green Original Palmolive dish soap. I was told not to use anything with a scent to it as it could cause problems internally. Using the water I am able to flush out my bowels so I don't have accidents. There are times when I don't wait long enough and it does cause problems but usually it's fairly effective. I have some issues with swimming that the doctors tell me I should not have. My stomach will pull in water through my belly button and act as if I'm doing my ace. To prevent this I've tried many things, the most successful for me was putting a tegaderm patch over my belly button so the water can't get in.

Around my 13th birthday I started having problems with my shunt. I went to my doctor and after running tests they decided to do surgery for replacement. I went in for one, a few days later ended up needing another one because something went wrong. My doctor thought I would be a good candidate for not needing a shunt by making canals in the brain and placing a thin tube through the canal called an "EVD drain" or external ventricular drain. They took my shunt out and put a tube in my head for 1-2 days to drain fluid. I had to go back into surgery to get the canals made for the fluid to flow through. I had the EVD for 2 days and ended up having to go back in for emergency surgery because it wasn't working properly and the fluid was just building up in my back. My back was hurting so bad because of the fluid back up, I had a headache, my vision was blurry, my mom even came to see me and I had no idea who anyone was. That's when she knew something was terribly wrong. My doctor came in and took me right back to surgery. This was my 4th surgery within a 2 week period. During surgery my shunt was put back in and everything was functioning fine, I stayed in the hospital for another day or two just to be sure everything was working properly. I was then sent on my way! I was happy to be back to my normal self!

At the age of 27 I had back surgery where they removed a portion of my spine because it was no longer functioning. My spine tried to attach itself to living tissue, tethering, causing pain and mobility problems. After and even for a few years before the surgery had I lost the ability to do steps on my own at all. It's frustrating to not be able to get up them on my own because I'm used to being able to do things and not have to ask for help. I am still able to walk down it's just going up that is the problem. For me to be able to manage the steps with my crutches someone has to be standing a step or two above me either holding my arm, depending how many steps there are, or allowing me to brace myself with my elbow against their hip for support. My arms, back and legs don't have the strength to pick me up anymore. I got rid of the pain I was having but I also lost the feeling and function in my right leg that I once had.

With all of these surgeries comes hospital stays. As a child I spent a lot of time in and out of the hospital whether it is being sick or because of surgery. Having my mom or someone with me made me feel a lot better.

Sometimes when a child is young they don't understand what is happening and why they need to be there so having someone can help them feel more comfortable and at ease.

I know it made me feel like everything was going to be okay. It taught me how to be brave because I didn't want them to see me scared. It also made the time go by faster because we would go for walks or to the playroom down the hall. It made me forget where I was for a while and helped me to relax.

The nurses play a big part in how the hospital stay will be. If I had nurses that were sweet and compassionate it made the stay a lot better. It gave me a sense of security that someone cares to take the time to listen and help with whatever I need.

Chapter Four
"What is a Shunt?"

What is a shunt? What does a shunt do? What is its purpose? Let's find out! Having a shunt doesn't usually stop me from doing things I love. I just have to be more cautious when doing things that may or may not cause me to hit my head. If I'm doing things where I'm being jolted or rough housing I may have had to be monitored more as a young child but as I got older I found what worked best for me and what I can or cannot do.

A shunt is a drain that is placed in the brain to drain cerebrospinal fluid from around the brain into another portion of the body. The body then disposes of the fluid in other ways such as absorption and emptying of the bladder. The reason for needing the shunt is because the body does not allow the fluid to flow as it should. Fluid build-up is called hydrocephalus or water on the brain. If left untreated there could be brain damage from the build-up of fluid.

Some of the symptoms of a shunt malfunction are headaches, vomiting, blurred vision and confusion. The signs and symptoms vary from one person to another but those are the most common. Parents tend to be more cautious of when their child has a headache due to the fact that it could mean a shunt malfunction. When symptoms appeared or lasted for a long period of time for me as a child, my mom would take me to see my neurologist and/or neurosurgeon, or go to the nearest emergency room. At the hospital a CT scan or MRI will be done to determine the cause of the symptoms. It will show if there's a blockage or any other malfunction.

Another way to test the shunt is to tap it. This is done by inserting a small needed into the shunt to obtain fluid to be tested for infection. Doctors can also see if the flow is possibly obstructed by doing a shunt tap. If there is an infection or blockage the individual will then be scheduled for an operation to fix the shunt. The patient can spend a few days in the hospital depending on the extent of the surgery and how well they recover. The recovery from shunt surgeries usually is not that extensive.

Some individuals actually need to have two shunts placed. The reason for this is sometimes the first one doesn't function properly or work as efficiently as it should. Placing two is useful in a more excessive build-up of cerebrospinal fluid. The most common place for a shunt to be placed is in the brain, draining down into the abdomen. Some may need it in their lung cavity or heart to eliminate fluid build-up

The shunt cannot be seen except sometimes the tubing can be visible under the skin in the neck or other parts of the body where the skin is not as thick; it may look just a little bumpy. It can be felt in the head as a bump under the skin. This bump tends to be squishy if pressed. Pressing the shunt too hard or hitting the head off of something can cause me to become lightheaded or dizzy. Often times this goes away within a few minutes. If there is pain around the shunt or lightheadedness or dizziness for an extended period of time this could mean something is wrong with the shunt itself and should be checked by a doctor.

My shunt has never stopped me from doing the things I wanted to do. I was still able to play with other kids, participate in activities with family. I just had to be a little more careful not to hit my head too hard, especially in the area of my shunt. Sometimes I hit my head because I'm not paying attention or I'm fooling around and sometimes it does cause me to get a little dizzy but it has never affected me that much where I couldn't do what I wanted. I have just had to learn my boundaries and what I'm capable of.

Chapter Five

"Living with Incontinence"

When dealing with paralysis it often means the struggle of incontinence as well. Incontinence could either be the bowels or bladder and most times it's both combined. This could be hard for a young child to cope with especially as they start going through school. Kids could tease them and often don't want to be around the individual. It takes a special person to truly understand what a person with incontinence experiences and goes through on a daily basis.

Most people with Spina Bifida do tend to be more self-conscious of themselves because of their incontinence. They're often afraid to go out for the day because they're afraid of having an accident. Not having control of something that most others do is a hard thing to accept. An individual dealing with these problems could also experience depression and anxiety because of their incontinence. They often feel ashamed of their problem because it's something they have no control over and often no warning that something is going to happen. They have a fear of being made fun of or punished because of their accident.

I know for me it's hard to deal with accidents sometimes. Especially if I'm out somewhere and something happens. I'm thankful to have family and friends who understand and will help me in any way possible to make the situation better. My friends and family always have ways to make me feel better whether it's making a joke of the situation or physically helping me clean up. If I didn't have that support I don't think things would be as easy as they are. We often take for granted the support we do have. It's important to be thankful and grateful for family and friends because not everyone is as lucky.

I've always had to take extra precautions when going out for the day; making sure I had supplies with me, and even a change of clothes. Dealing with incontinence is not an easy thing, just for the simple fact that it could change day to day. One day things may be fine but the next our body's will act up and cause problems. This is a struggle for more individuals than most realize.

When I got my ACE surgery my life changed as far as having to carry a lot of supplies. My accidents lessened, I felt better about myself and was just happier. I didn't have to carry around a ton of extra clothes and pads. I could feel confident leaving the house for the day with maybe 1-2 pads and a pair of underwear not having to worry about having a problem.

My incontinence has gotten to be a little bit of an issue as I've gotten older. I find myself carrying more supplies with me again just to be on the safe side. If I'm just out for a few hours with a friend or something I will just carry a small pouch with some catheters, gloves, pads and maybe a change of underwear. However, if I know I'm going somewhere for the day I will carry a backpack that I can put more supplies in and keep a full change of clothes if needed. Being prepared will help you build confidence and feel more at ease. Sometimes I don't need everything I bring with me but having it I feel like gives me more security knowing I have everything I will need for the day.

I'm still getting used to having to carry things with me again but I have found discreet ways that work for me. I have a small bag that attaches to the front of my wheelchair behind my legs that nobody can really see but it's big enough for me to keep some extra supplies handy for times of need. I also have a backpack I take to work that I can put extra clothes in as well as supplies. There is nothing wrong with having to carry personal items all the time. If it helps with independence it's worth it! There are many different things that can be used to carry supplies. I have found so many stylish bags that are perfect for carrying supplies and nobody would even know the difference!

Chapter Six
"A Mix of Medications"

Most individuals with Spina Bifida need to take daily medications including myself. Some of those are bladder control and a form of pain relief. Most of us deal with pain pretty much daily. One medication that can help with that is Neurontin. This medication helps to calm down the nerves in the body to ease pain. I also take over the counter medications daily for pain such as Tylenol or Motrin from a local store. These will reduce inflammation and relax muscles. They are often what will help me to function throughout the day with minimal pain.

Bladder incontinence is common in Spina Bifida so medication is often needed to help prevent accidents caused by bladder spasms and weak muscles. Sometimes more than one medication needs to be used to resolve problems with incontinence such as Imipramine and other bladder control medication. There are also preventatives that can be used to prevent urinary tract infections. Other medications could be for bowel incontinence, or other stomach problems.

There are so many medications that can be used to treat different problems. Spina Bifida has a wide range of difficulties that vary from one person to another. Medication treatment varies so much because everyone is so different and what works for one may not work for another. Finding the regimen that works for me has made dealing with my problems a lot easier by lessening my incontinence and pain altogether.

Knowing my medication and when to take it is important. I was taught young what the medication is, when I was supposed to take it and why I had to take a medication. This made me become more responsible. By the time I got to school I knew "this is what I'm supposed to take and this is when I'm supposed to take it. This was helpful when I needed to take medication at school. I was able to communicate with nurses and other staff to tell them what I needed and when. A daily pill case with slots for different days and times is a tool that can be used to teach children what pills they're supposed to take at specific times of the day.

Every morning I take 3 bladder medications, 2 are for control and one is an infection preventative. I also have Neurontin for my back pain, Metoprolol for high blood pressure, a multivitamin as well as an allergy medication for seasonal allergies. Sometimes in the morning I do need to add Tylenol or Motrin but not always. In the afternoon I have to take 2 more of my bladder medications. This is to overlap the morning dose and increase control.

At night I take Neurontin again as well as Tylenol or Motrin if needed.

Chapter Seven

"Gaining Control and Being Discreet"

Gaining control is a big achievement for anyone dealing with a disability. Some things that can be done to gain control are surgeries and therapy. Making changes and adjustments as a child may make life as an adult a little easier. If something doesn't feel right, talk to a doctor or a family member right away. As we get older problems become harder to fix so taking care of them as a young child will benefit us in the long run.

Children and adults sometimes need special supplies to deal with certain problems so being discreet is something that could help make things easier, whether it's carrying personal supplies (pads, catheters, diapers etc.) in a special bag that no one else would know what it is or even just saying something simple like "I will be back I need to take care of something." Giving whoever we are with enough information that they won't worry where we are but also keeping it private enough where we don't feel embarrassed or out of place is important to living an independent life with Spina Bifida.

Learning how to take care of our bodies on our own is another way we can be discreet and gain control. Whether it's getting a shower or taking care of a problem while we are out knowing how to manage it on our own will give us more confidence and show people that we can do this! I can understand the embarrassment of having to tell someone about an accident and needing help. There is nothing wrong with needing help.

Over the years I have struggled a lot with incontinence. I have felt defeated, I felt bad because I couldn't help the things that were happening. These feelings are normal! Finding ways to make these feelings less bothersome will boost confidence and make things so much easier emotionally, knowing that it's not our fault. We're doing all we can to handle the situation and take care of it. Being open about struggles, talking to family and friends, or maybe even a teacher or counselor is always best. Holding it in will only hurt in the long run. Talk about feelings and take control!

One big way to gain control of our disability is acceptance. Accept things for how they are and make the necessary changes to make things better for us. It can be hard to accept things sometimes because we may not completely understand what's going on ourselves. A lot of people feel ashamed or like they've done something wrong because things just aren't going their way. Feeling sorry for ourselves and just a little down is okay as long as we pick ourselves back up and move on from the situation. Figuring out what works best for us and take things one day at a time. In time we figure out our own little way to handle problems and find ways that make our life easier for us.

Chapter Eight

"The Struggle with Mobility"

Mobility is usually a problem for those with Spina Bifida. Some need braces to keep their legs from bending or just to support their ankles. Others need crutches, walkers or canes for stability. There are some that can't use any of those and rely completely on a wheelchair. Some are able to walk with minimal bracing and no aids while others may not be able to move or support themselves with their legs at all. All of this depends on the level of Spina Bifida they have.

The level of Spina Bifida is determined by the location of the opening on the spine at birth. The lower the defect the less paralysis there will be which means the individual is usually able to walk on their own with minimal bracing and aids. If the opening is higher it's going to cause more paralysis which means the individual is going to need more support when trying to walk if they're able to walk at all.

I can walk with crutches and leg braces. My left brace goes to my upper thigh and the right just supports the ankle and foot. As a child it was easy for me to get up with my crutches and go wherever I wanted to. I used to walk all day when I was in junior high. Elementary school I used my chair because it was easier for me to keep up with other kids. High school I used my chair for all 4 years because the school was so big and crowded; I wasn't able to manage with my crutches.

Some people do feel more comfortable using their wheelchairs because they feel freer. They feel like they're able to be more involved with activities because they can use their hands to do things and still be stable. Also in a wheelchair they're quicker. They're able to push themselves with their arms quicker to where they want or need to go.

I am relying on my wheelchair a lot more now than I did when I was younger. It is very frustrating not being able to do the things I used to, I oftentimes wonder why? I get upset, I get down on myself, I do get days where I just want to be left alone but I'm slowly getting more comfortable with the fact that things are changing for me. I am finding that a lot of things are actually easier in my chair than they would have been with my crutches. I feel like I'm more free in my chair, yes it's still hard to accept the fact I can't do what I used to but I'm slowly becoming more comfortable with where my life is going and who I'm becoming. My mom has always told me she would fight as long as I am willing but she has said to me "I think it's time" and I'm beginning to think she's right. At 31 years old I don't want to be told that, I don't want to feel like I'm just giving up but she is right. If I'm by myself there's so much I can't do if I'm on my crutches because I need the help. If I'm in my chair I can do so much more. I'm free!

When in my chair or sitting in general I'm able to be more involved with family and friends. I am able to help them with things because my hands aren't tied up with the crutches. Being in my chair more and not walking as much has made my arms weaker than they used to be which makes things harder but I still feel free when I'm using my chair. I can reach things I wouldn't normally reach with my crutches. I can carry things I wouldn't normally be able to carry. There are so many things I can accomplish by using my chair. Yes, it's frustrating for me because I want to be able to walk, I don't want to give that up but at the same time I have to listen to my body. I think that's a big problem for everyone they don't want to feel like they're giving up or being defeated so they don't listen to what their body is telling them.

If we don't listen to our bodies and keep pushing we could ultimately do more damage in the long run. If something hurts, we have to stop; take a break. I think what we don't always think about is whatever we're doing we can always go back to later. If we push ourselves to hard we could be down longer than if we'd just stopped for a second and took a break.

I know how it feels to want to keep going. We want to be just like everyone else but what we also have to understand is that our bodies are different. They're not built like everyone else so it's going to take more time for us to do tasks and get certain places but that's okay!

Chapter Nine

"Keeping a Balanced Diet and Weight"

Keeping a balanced diet is important for anyone. But for someone with a disability gaining unnecessary weight could prevent them from being able to walk or move at all. Ones who walk with crutches, canes or walkers need to be especially careful because the extra weight could make it difficult or impossible for them to continue to use their arms for those aids. The shoulders and back can only stand so much strain. As individuals get older their muscles tend to get weaker so having the extra weight put on them is not really a good idea.

Making sure we are eating the right foods and exercising as much as possible is sometimes difficult. For some who are in wheelchairs, it may be difficult for them to do certain exercises in order to lose the weight. Paralysis can also cause problems in trying to get the weight off. The paralyzed portion of the body often does not lose the weight as well, if at all as other parts of the body that are still mobile. Anyone with lowered mobility is more at risk for being obese and having difficulty losing the weight. All of this has to do with muscle strength. Making sure we are staying in a healthy weight range and staying as active as possible is very important.

Some ways to stay active are lifting weights, sit ups if possible and walking. For anyone who cannot walk, doing wheelchair pushups can help to keep the strength of the upper body and help to burn calories as well. Twisting from side to side and holding for a couple seconds in the wheelchair will help with abdominal muscles and help with keeping them in shape. Stretching from side to side is another way to make sure the core muscles are strong. Doing these exercises with weights, starting off small, will help strengthen the muscles and also help with toning of the muscles.

Individuals that are able to get on the floor doing push-ups or sit-ups will help keep the arms and core muscles strong. Pushing yourself around whether it's inside or out is a great way to build up arm strength as well. It doesn't matter how far they go or how long they're out, short periods and distances everyday work best eventually building up to going farther longer.

When I was younger I was always on the go whether it was in my chair or walking with my crutches I would not sit still. I wanted to be just like everyone else. In school in my younger years I would use my chair all the time so for gym the teacher would always have things for me to do. I played basketball with the other kids; I played dodgeball and even baseball.

Anything everyone else was doing my teacher would give me the chance to try too.

As a child I didn't like being confined to my chair, let's be honest what kid does! I had the ability to get where I wanted to go by walking so I didn't see a need for the chair. I would use it for going out somewhere if it was an excessive amount of walking but for the most part I used my crutches. This was beneficial because it helped me maintain my weight.

At home I had younger cousins so we were always outside playing games. I even had a Barbie jeep that I could drive around. My cousins hated when I got that out because I would chase them with it. We would play hide and seek, as well as other games. Don't ever let someone tell you that just because you have limitations you can't stay active! We can do anything if we put our mind to it and try!

As I got older I've had to rely on my chair so I've had to come up with other ways to stay in shape. It's been a struggle because my muscles are no longer as strong as they used to be. I found that my diet has been the key to maintaining my weight and staying healthy. Eating the same way you did when you were active is not always a good thing because your body isn't moving and burning as many calories so what you eat turns into fat because you're not burning it off.

Over the years I've struggled with my weight, especially as I got older and my mobility changed. The things I used to be able to eat I couldn't anymore because I wasn't burning off the calories that I had been when I was able to walk more. This has made it hard for me because once I gained the weight I noticed it was even harder to lose it again. The lack of mobility and movement has made it almost impossible.

If someone lets things get out of control as a child it will be hard and even impossible to ever go back to what they were when they're older. The more weight they gain as kids the harder their adult lives will be.

Chapter Ten
"Living with Allergies"

Many individuals struggle with allergies. With Spina Bifida there are many other allergies that many may not even think would be a problem. One of the most common is an allergy to Latex which is often found in rubber. Latex can also be associated with different foods. Many with this allergy cannot eat things like banana, avocado, kiwi, cantaloupe and honeydew. These are just a few of the many foods that someone with a latex allergy should be careful of. There are certain proteins that latex produces and these proteins are also found in these foods.

Someone with allergies should always carry Benadryl or an Epipen with them. The Epipen would require a prescription from the child's pediatrician. This will be useful if a reaction occurs. Many of these things will only last so long so always be cautious of the dates on bottles and boxes.

Reactions may vary from person to person but common symptoms include; trouble breathing, hives, and being itchy. Some allergies could become severe enough to actually need medical attention. If this should happen it is important to act quickly. If Benadryl and/or other forms of allergy medication have been used but are not helping 911 should be called immediately.

As a person grows and changes their allergies could change as well. Just because something didn't affect someone before doesn't mean it won't affect them now. Be cautious of balloons, gloves, and even band aids. These often contain latex that could cause a reaction.

As a child I had a lot of problems with certain tapes and bandages. I would get red and little hives around the area of contact. As I've gotten older my allergies have changed. I never had a problem with fruits as a child but as I've grown I've noticed changes in what I can and cannot eat. I can no longer eat bananas or cantaloupe, because my mouth and throat start to itch whenever I do eat them. Balloons cause me to get itchy if I touch them. If I'm in close contact with balloons and can smell the latex I could even have a little trouble breathing.

Once after a surgery I had been given morphine to help control my pain. It was a medication I've had before but for an unknown reason it caused a severe reaction this particular time. The doctors had it going through my IV so all I had to do was press a button when I had pain and it would give the medication to me at a certain time. Not long after having it in I started to get itchy and not be able to breathe. It started as just being tingly then slowly progressed to being itchy all over my whole body. I told my mom that I didn't feel right so she got my nurse. When the nurse came in to check on me they immediately disconnected the morphine from the IV. My whole body was itchy and my throat felt like it was tightening up. They gave me another medication such as Benadryl or another antihistamine to counteract the reaction. Within a few minutes I was starting to feel better, the itching had subsided and I felt like I could breathe again.

After surgery the surgeon will sometimes put steri-strips over the incision to help it heal depending on the location. These are little white strips that are glued over the incision to secure it sometimes in the place of stitches. I had them on my stomach after a shunt revision and not long after I started to get itchy and a rash. I did not take them off right away because you're told not to peel them. From not taking the strips off it only got worse. It got to the point I actually had blisters all over my stomach. We don't know if it was a reaction to the glue or the strips but I was not allowed to use either of them again. After going in to see my doctor he gently peeled the strips off and cleaned the skin to prevent infection. My skin was a mess. Thankfully it cleared up within a few days after removal.

Being aware of my surroundings was always very important. I had to be prepared for the unknown. It's helpful to be prepared if an outing is planned for an extended period of time and access to medication quickly may be limited. Packing Benadryl or whatever else may be needed in case of a reaction is very important.

Some allergic reactions could be life threatening. It was always crucial for me to know my body and how much I was able to tolerate before things got too far. I was always told that if I felt I was in danger of something life threatening I should call 911 immediately. Thankfully I've never had to but it's a good piece of advice for someone who could have these problems pop up so randomly.

Chapter Eleven

"Having Confidence and a Positive Attitude"

Life with a disability can be very difficult. I have had to deal with surgeries, trouble in school, and having to adapt to a world that wasn't built for me, among many other things. The way it turns out is our attitude toward things. In order to have the life we deserve we should be positive.

Having a positive attitude has helped me to see the good in situations rather than the bad. It helped me to be more confident in myself. It'll show the world that I know what I'm doing; I know what I want to achieve. It's hard coming out of your shell sometimes especially when everything else around you is not made for you. Pushing me to be the best person of myself has been the key to my success.

Asking for help when needed is okay. It shows that I know my limits; I know what I can and cannot do on my own. Admitting I need help shows that I am brave enough to stand up and admit that I can't do something. It doesn't show failure, it shows confidence and bravery.

Independence will also help me in the real world. As mentioned it is okay to need help but showing people that I can do things for myself is also important. Understandably many will still need assistance but doing as much as you can for yourself is just as important. It gives me confidence to take on other tasks I wouldn't normally try to take on. It will prove to me and the world that even with a disability I can accomplish anything. Especially when I look back at something I've done and think "wow I did that myself."

Maybe the individual can't live alone, maybe they can't do much for themselves or maybe they just need a little help; this is all okay! I have learned so many ways around obstacles that so many people have told me I couldn't do. It all comes down to my attitude and my outlook on things. If I'm positive and optimistic I noticed that things will turn out better than if I'm down on myself and doubtful.

Many people will have negative comments about me, maybe I don't hear them; maybe I do, regardless I don't let that stop me from doing what I want to in my life. This is my time to shine! I have had negative comments said to and about me my whole life. Did it bother me? Yes. Did it make me doubt my self-worth? Yes. Did it make me wonder why I wasn't good enough? Yes. I have had all these feelings but I was able to push through them. I was able to say "you know, what I'm not going to let this bother me, I am good enough." It's hard I will admit but with strength, courage and support I made it through!

My family and friends are what got me through a lot of my dark times. Without them I wouldn't be the person I am today. I often saw leaning on people for support as being a weak person but in reality it's the complete opposite. Being able to admit that I need the help and that I can't do some things has made me a stronger person. It has pushed me to work harder at achieving more on my own. But sometimes we do need that helping hand to say "hey it's okay we got this together." Just because we are strong people does not mean we have to face everything alone.

There were times when I fought things alone. I didn't tell anyone how I felt or what was going on. This only made situations harder on me because I felt like I didn't have anyone to lean on. I found as I got older it was better for me to be more open about things that were going on in my life. No matter how hard or personal it was, talking to someone makes it easier to deal with. I would get a different perspective and maybe open my eyes to something I hadn't noticed before.

Chapter Twelve
"Having Family Support"

Having a supportive family is very important and encouraging. Having someone to ask for help or talk to makes someone feel loved and cared for, not just when they have a disability but anytime at all. Sometimes having a disability can make someone feel like they're not good enough, it can make them feel helpless and alone. Having someone to confide in on those days will help work through them a lot better.

My family has always been very supportive of me and my decisions. They have helped to guide me down the right path and have even stepped in when they felt the need. Having people that will allow me to try things for myself but also help me when it's necessary are the types of people I need in my life. Not someone who's overbearing and treats me like a child or someone who can't do anything for themselves at all.

Family has been there to guide me while allowing me to try my wings. Sometimes I need to stand up for myself and say "no, this does not work for me" or "no, this is what I want." It may not always be easy and it may even hurt a few feelings but in the end what's best for me is what's important. Nobody else has to live my life except me!

Knowing I am capable of accomplishing something for me is the best feeling, also knowing that if I need it I have the help there. Having at least one person I know is always there has helped me succeed even more in life. It gave me that necessary push and encouragement that I can do anything I put my mind to. This is my life and my time to shine.

Sometimes family can be a little too protective. Sometimes they don't allow me to spread my wings as much as I'd like and that's okay. One thing I have to remember is; just as I'm learning so are they! They're learning how to let me be free. They're learning that I can do a lot for myself. Maybe they're a first time parent to a child with a disability. Or a first time parent period. No matter what the case is learning to be patient with family is important. They want what's best for the individual! I have also had to keep in mind that maybe my family sees dangers that I'm not opening my eyes to. Just because I want to do something doesn't always mean it's safe for me.

With time and patience children can achieve anything they want to. Just because a child has a disability doesn't mean they can't do things that are fun. It just may take some time and adaption for them to be able to accomplish it, and that's okay!

Believe it or not, kids will say when they can't do something or if something is not right. Most times they're just trying to keep up with kids their own age; they're trying to fit in! That's all kids want! They want to feel like they belong with kids their age; they don't want to feel left out.

As a kid I always wanted to be able to at least say I tried. I never wanted to be the kid that gave up and relied on other people for everything. My whole life was a struggle between surgeries and everything I've had to deal with. But at the same time I had a lot of success. I was a dancer for a few years. I had recitals that I was a part of; being on that stage doing the things that other girls my age were doing was something I always wanted. I always did what I could to fit in. I never wanted anyone to think I couldn't do things other kids were doing just because I have a disability.

After surgeries I would struggle a lot especially as I got older, moving around and being mobile was difficult. Walking with my crutches and trying to go up the stairs is hard for me normally but after surgery it does become even more difficult. I will never forget a few days after my most recent back surgery I was out with my sister just a few days after being home from the hospital and she gave me the biggest compliment anyone could ever give. She told me that she was proud of me because she could tell I still struggled but I kept trying and was doing well. Those simple words are what will stay with me forever. She may not remember what she said but I DO! She has been a big part of whom I am today and why I push so hard to be the best I can be.

When I would have surgeries or need any kind of bandage change my sister was always right there wanting to help. Some of the worst wounds I've had never seemed to phase her. She would do whatever she had to do and didn't ever complain. When I had a port in my chest due to a bone infection she would always tell me she wanted to help me give myself the antibiotics. No matter what time of day it was she insisted on doing it for me.

I have a younger cousin who is 3 now. He's the smartest little boy I know. He is very attentive to me and wanting me to do things with him. He knows the crutches are mine to help me walk so he'll pick them up and give them to me sometimes. He hasn't ever tried to play with them like most kids would. He doesn't look at me differently like other kids would. If he wants me to play he tells me to sit down first. He has even asked me to take him to the bathroom. When his mom said it was hard for me to do it he insisted that I take him anyway. He holds doors open for me and even tries to push me when I'm in my chair, which he's only seen twice.

I feel like his reaction is because he's grown up with it and doesn't know any different. He never asks me why, he always treats me like everyone else. It's so nice to feel accepted. You could tell he truly loves being around me. A lot of kids tend to shy away because they don't know what things are and to them it seems strange but he doesn't. He runs right up to me wanting hugs and kisses. Sometimes if I tell him I can't do something he'll say "yes Tillie!" He's the little push I need to keep active because if I'm not active I won't be able to play with him like he wants me to.

He will pull out chairs for me and bring things to me he wants me to play with, such as puzzles. He has seen two of my other friends who are also in wheelchairs and he acted the same way toward them. It was as if he didn't even see the chair. He held doors open for us, scared us and pretended to tickle us. He is the sweetest and most helpful little boy I know.

Chapter Thirteen

"Life Altering Modifications"

Many children and adults with Spina Bifida require special modifications to live a day to day life. Whether that's ramps, lower countertops, modifications to a vehicle or something as simple as a bath chair. These are just a few of the many modifications an individual may need. Getting in and out of the home might require a ramp where there are stairs. Maybe they're thinking about driving but don't have use of their legs. Modifications to the vehicle would be necessary to make driving possible.

Making adjustments made to daily life could help them become a better and more independent individual. Knowing the right individuals to contact to get these things done is important. Maybe it's reaching out to a local church, the community or going through an organization.

Many organizations will come to the home and assess what's there and what needs to be done. A lot of them are funded through the government and may only require minimal cost to the individual if anything at all. They can do things as little as bathroom modifications to installing a ramp outside the home. I have personally just started getting things done to my home to make things easier for me and my family.

I've had people come out to assess my outside to get a ramp and sidewalk installed so I can have access to my home with use of my wheelchair. We have to go through the back to do this because our front is not wheelchair friendly. They are putting in a sidewalk that will take me from the front of the house to the back door where there will be a ramp going in so I won't have to deal with any steps at all. This is exciting for me because I feel like I will finally get my independence back. Right now I need help getting in and out of my home because we have steps out front to get in from outside. With the ramp and sidewalk installed I will be able to access my home without ever having to navigate stairs. This will give me more freedom and independence in the future when I'm out with friends or just want to sit outside. It will also increase my independence because I'll be able to accomplish this myself and not have to ask for help.

I'm also looking into getting a bathroom installed on the lower level of my home. Right now I'm living with family so I have to go up and down stairs to use the bathroom. We are trying to make things more accessible and private for me; also having friends over will be easier because they won't have to worry about stairs either. Most of my friends are in chairs so hanging out with them is sometimes difficult or impossible at my house because of the stairs. Having these adaptations done will help make things more accessible for them as well.

Vehicle modifications are helpful to anyone with limited or no use of their legs and feet. This will allow the driver to use their hands to drive instead of having to use pedals. Hand controls would be applied to the steering wheel that would control the gas and break of the vehicle. There are knobs that can be put on the steering wheel as well to help with making turns and make it more comfortable for the driver. Chair lifts can be installed on certain vehicles that will lift the individuals chair for them. Normally the chair would go up to a compartment on top of the vehicle. The lift would be controlled by a remote that could be kept inside the vehicle for easy access.

There are so many things that can be done to make living with a disability a little easier. Stair lifts can be installed inside the home where ramps would not be possible to navigate stairs. This device will take the individual up and down the stairs either in their chair or seated in a chair depending on what kind of lift is installed. This allows the individual to navigate the stairs safely and also allows them the freedom to carry items up and down without fear of falling or dropping anything. When not in use the lift can be folded up and put out of the way of anyone else who may need to use the stairs.

Chapter Fourteen
"Facing the World"

Going out on our own and facing the world can be scary! Fear of the unknown! Having a lot of encouragement and support from family and friends is very important. There's a sense of freedom and independence we feel when we get out on our own. It takes a lot of courage and responsibility to be successful living alone.

Making sure we have all finances in order and of course have a house or apartment to move into before making that big leap to independence! I feel like the hardest part for me would be trying to juggle my finances. I am a very conscious person when it comes to money and my spending. A big part of going on my own is feeling ready. If I'm not ready or feel unsure I won't do it.

Whether it is doors not being automatic or things being just a little too high we always have to adapt to our surroundings. When looking for a home we have to pay attention to all of the little details. The doors, countertops, stairs and shower are just a few things to look at. Depending on the style and size of the wheelchair certain doorways may not be wide enough to fit through. Countertops may need to be lowered to be able to reach, taking into consideration a sink that is open underneath so the chair can roll right under it. These are just a few of the many things to take into consideration when looking for a home.

Shopping can be a hassle sometimes for anyone but it's especially difficult for someone with a disability because often times we are smaller than the average person especially when it comes to height. Being in a wheelchair we are not really able to push a cart and ourselves with ease. If it had to be done it could be but it takes a lot longer than anyone else would. It would also be hard to try to hold our groceries while pushing our chair.

Finding ways to fix these problems is important. Maybe it's carrying a bag, maybe attaching something to our wheelchair. Whatever it is that works for the individual is what's important. For me since I'm still able to walk a little bit I'm able to use the motorized carts. This is helpful because I'm able to put things in the basket and drive at the same time. But not all of us have that option, finding other ways that work best is essential.

A big problem most people face is parking. Whether the spaces aren't big enough or maybe there isn't one close enough it's always a hassle. Having a handicap sign is important because it allows us to park in the spaces that are just a little bit closer. But what if those spaces are not available? Sometimes we go somewhere and there aren't any handicap spaces left so what do we do? If the use of a wheelchair is an option parking at the other end of the parking lot away from other cars and able to get our chair out safely. If use of a wheelchair isn't an option finding the closest spot available is something to consider which would eliminate walking as far. Knowing our limits will help in the decision on which parking spot is chosen. Choosing one further away without the ability to do the walking wouldn't be a good option.

I would say the biggest problem for me with being out would be the restrooms. Sometimes the handicap stalls aren't big enough to fit a wheelchair comfortably. There isn't enough room to really lay out all of our supplies to use the bathroom. I often find myself using my shirt and holding it in my teeth just to be able to hold everything. For those that may even need a little more help and actually need someone in the stall with them it's sometimes nearly impossible because the stalls just aren't large enough. Sometimes it requires physically taking the individuals wheelchair out of the stall just so the person trying to help can fit in.

When I'm out shopping at an outlet or something I need to be very careful and pay attention to the sidewalks. I've noticed that sometimes they don't have a handicap outlet for us to get from one sidewalk to another. This makes it difficult and dangerous because most times the individual ends up having to go out onto the road or a busy parking lot just to get where they need to go. Many times my family has taken me off the curbs by tipping my chair back and rolling me off the curb with the big tires but if we're by ourselves that isn't an option. Even with the help of someone that could be difficult and dangerous. There's a risk falling out of our chair and getting hurt as well as getting hit by another vehicle.

Public transportation can be a problem if we can't find the right van or bus to ride. Finding one with a wheelchair lift is sometimes very difficult and actually requires going through special companies that are specifically for handicap transportation. There are agencies around that could help with this; we just have to know where to look. Try calling the local bus station to see if they have accommodations or going online to search for handicap transportation in the area.

I have been using a company for right around 3 years now to get to work every day. They are reliable and very helpful when it comes to my needs. They pick me up in the morning and come right to my door to help me carry my things. They take me up on the wheelchair lift since I can't use the stairs. In the winter it can be a bit more of a problem. I don't walk very well on the snow and ice so it requires them to be a little bit more of assistance to me. In times like that they will hold my arm to stabilize me from falling. I haven't had any problems with them doing things for me which is nice. It's so hard to find people that are so willing to help anyway they can so I'm very appreciative of what they do.

As we go out and face the world we will run into a lot of inconsiderate people. We can't let them get to us. It's going to be hard, we are probably going to want to make a comment back at them but really it's not worth the time or frustration. It's not going to change how anyone acts to another person. The most important thing to realize is that their actions are not a reflection on us. It doesn't matter how nice we are to a person or how much we do for someone if that person wants to be mean and nasty that's just how they're going to be. It may hurt our feelings and make us wonder what we've done wrong but we can't let it affect the people we are. Tell yourself that you're going to be the bigger person.

I have a few friends that live on their own but the one who has been the most help and most open is Brian. We've been friends for 10 years and he has answered a lot of questions I've had about living on my own. He has taken me to his house to show me how it's set up just so I can get ideas for when the time comes for me to do it. He also shows me things with driving so when I'm ready to get my license and start the process myself I kind of know what I'm looking for and what questions to ask. He has told me it is not easy but worth it. He owns his own house, drives his own car, works and even does his own shopping. Yes, he has family to help but he does the majority of it alone. I find that amazing. I have always said I wanted to but I wasn't ever sure I could. Watching him and seeing how he does things shows me that maybe down the road I can too.

Caitlin though she still lives at home is another person I have learned a lot from. She is able to cook for herself and do her own laundry. Seeing how she's able to do these things gives me ideas about how I could do them one day too! We have been best friends since 2001 and still going strong. Having friends like that is important because it gives you someone to turn to when things get tough.

Over the past few years Brian and Caitlin have been the friends I rely on the most. They get what I go through on a daily basis. They know the struggles and the let downs.

When I'm with either one of them we always work well as a team. Usually what one person can't do another has the ability to. Brian and I have accomplished getting my wheelchair in and out of his vehicle by ourselves multiple times. I'm sure we have been doubted but we made it work. Was it easy? No, but the satisfaction of saying we did this by ourselves was worth it! Caitlin and I are able to spend a whole day out shopping after being dropped off somewhere with no help. We help each other with things in the house, sometimes even personal problems. She has helped me take care of personal problems so many times and has never complained. These are the kind of people we need in our life!

These two are just 2 examples of individuals being able to face the world with a disability. They both push me to do things to make me more independent. To me they're just 2 reasons I will never give up! Just because things are hard doesn't mean it's over!

Chapter Fifteen

"Being Accepted: Fitting In"

Fitting in with the outside world with a disability is always hard. Maybe it's getting teased; maybe it is feeling left out, no matter what the situation, fitting in is never easy. We can feel like an outcast, like we just don't fit in. Having the right people by our side is going to help give a feeling of being included and like we belong.

What we are all doing is trying to fit into a world that wasn't built for us. We will need to come up with our own ways of accomplishing what we want to do. People may say it's the wrong way of doing it but if it works for us that's all that matters. It's our life we need to live it to the fullest.

I have attended several camps that are specifically meant for anyone with a disability. To me they're the best places in the world because I feel normal. I feel like I can do anything because everyone else is just like me. It often takes teamwork from another wheelchair user to accomplish something but we're still able to get it done ourselves. The counselors are always amazed at what we are able to accomplish on our own. A lot of them are ready to jump right in and do something until they realize that we can do it ourselves. I've been told many times by counselors that I amaze them because I'm able to achieve things that most others wouldn't even attempt.

At camp I feel free and happy because I don't feel different; I am just like everyone else. People accept me for who I am and they don't see me as a disabled person because they're just like me. I don't feel the need to explain anything to any of my camp friends because they understand what I go through. They all know the struggles and what comes along with having a disability. When I'm at camp I'm not afraid to try new things because I know it's safe for me.

We do things that normally people like us wouldn't be able to do in the real world. Some of those things include rock wall climbing and zip lining. I have tried climbing at other places but it wasn't like being at camp. We're still strapped to harnesses but it's ALL us. At camp we have someone on the other end of that rope helping to pull us when we need the extra push. I know it's not actually doing it all ourselves but making it to the top of that wall gives me such a sense of accomplishment. Hearing my friends cheering for me at the bottom gives me a rush that's hard to explain.

Zip lining is another activity that I would never be able to do in the real world. We are strapped into a seat harness, which is basically a wheelchair cushion with harness straps. There is a platform that we're wheeled up onto and once secured we're on our way. It's such an amazing feeling to be going through the air knowing that you're doing this yourself. It gives me a feeling of accomplishment.

Going through school could be a little tough. Especially as we get into junior high or high school. One would think it should get easier as we get older but in fact it gets harder. Young kids don't care what we look like or what we're capable of. All they want is a friend. Older kids can judge, they can be cruel and say mean things. Having a strong mental state and knowing it's not our fault is the most important thing we can do. Showing them what we're capable of and letting them know that we can do almost anything they can do will really help when dealing with the bullies. Whether it's in gym class or just general conversation being confident and showing them that we can be just like them is what will make them change their mind. They will see what strong fun individuals we are capable of being and want to know more about us!

Outings with friends could be pretty stressful for some individuals simply because we tend to worry about having an accident or needing help with something while we're out. It's important to find the right people and be honest with them as hard as that may be. Showing them our confidence and perseverance will tell that person what strong individuals we truly are. Have fun, go on that shopping outing, do what makes you happy. If they're a true friend they will love us for the honest and confident individuals we truly can be.

As a child and even still today one of the things I love to do and wish I got to do a lot more is horseback riding. The freedom I feel on the back of that horse is unreal. Most people think that just because I have a disability I shouldn't be doing that but it's actually very good for you. With the right trainer and safety precautions horseback riding is very therapeutic. It strengthens the core muscles because you're using them for balance and will also help with leg muscles if you have the ability to use your legs. There are special straps that can be used to hold the legs if the rider doesn't have the ability to use them to hold themselves. I know of many people who rode horses regularly and even went as far as competition. Something like that is a huge way to show people what you're capable of. Not only riding the horse but going on to compete is amazing.

At one of the camps I attended we had a day where we were just in the pool all day doing different activities. Whether it was swimming, kayaking or goofing off. They even had scuba diving for us to try. There was a pool that was a lot deeper than your typical pool so they would get scuba instructors to gear up and take us down to play games. That was something I always enjoyed because I love being in the water and trying different things.

At the bottom of the pool they had tic tac toe and playing catch with foam torpedoes. The first year I tried it I was afraid and changed my mind but after seeing all my friends do it, it was something I wanted to try again. Once I got over the fear of actually going down to the bottom it was an amazing experience. Being under water I have more freedom to move around and let the water carry me. It strengthens my arm and stomach muscles as well as my back muscles as I move through the water. Being under the water we found different ways to communicate with our friends and the instructors. They even had boards that were magnetic we could write on to tell someone a message.

All of these things and so much more are some of the many reasons I have returned to camp year after year. I felt comfortable there with friends who understood what I went through as well as counselors that I knew wouldn't let anything bad happen to us. All of these years going were some of the best experiences of my life. Going home every year my family couldn't believe the things I told them I did. They would often ask "how were you able to do that when you don't have use of your legs" or whatever the activity required. I would explain to them how we did things and they were just in awe. Most of these activities were things my family never thought I would be able to accomplish. Being able to prove it to them through pictures and videos would always give me the best feeling of accomplishment. It was my way of saying "yes this is something I can do believe it or not."

Chapter Sixteen
"School with a Disability"

Attending school with a disability could be harder for some than others. Some may have to get up extra early just to be ready on time because of morning rituals. Others need more of a push to get up and go due to anxiety problems and being afraid of being mistreated.

The teachers play a big part in a child being excited to go to school. It takes a special person to be able to handle an individual with a disability. The teacher needs to be patient, attentive, and caring. Encouraging the student to try their best at something has an impact on how the child will feel about school. Having a positive experience with the teachers and the students can change the whole experience of school for the child.

Fellow classmates also play a part in a child being excited or the opposite, nervous about attending school. If the kids are nice and friendly then chances are the child will warm up quickly and have more fun. Feeling welcome and being asked to participate with other kids is a huge battle for children with a disability. Often kids can be mean to someone who is different than they are. Having this kind of experience can discourage a child from wanting to go to school and can even show them that all kids are the same when they're really not.

If a child needs to take any type of medication while at school it's important for them to understand what they take, when they take it and why, as well as dosage. It's important because they need to be able to tell their teachers when it's time for the medication. It's also beneficial for the teacher to understand the importance of the medication the child needs to take. They need to understand what the medication is for and what its purpose is. Hopefully in explaining this it will enforce the importance of the child having that particular medication at a particular time.

Limitations can really be frustrating to a younger child, especially when they see other kids doing different things and they can't. Explaining to a child why they shouldn't do something is a good way to teach them about being safe. It's not telling them they're incapable of doing a particular activity, it's just saying it may not be safe for them. Giving a child another activity that they are capable of doing will help them to not feel so left out. Maybe even asking another classmate to play with them for a while will build their spirits and make them feel like they're more involved.

Transportation is always a problem for someone with a disability. They either need a family member to bring them to school with a special vehicle or most are able to ride on handicap busses. These busses normally have a driver with an aide to help with loading the students on and off the bus. There are normally only 1 to 3 kids on these busses at one time. Once at school there is usually another aide waiting for the child to arrive. If the child uses the bus to get home they either need to make sure there is someone home to get them off the bus or sometimes they are capable of being home alone. The individual just might need assistance getting into the home. Sometimes this isn't allowed though depending on the busing company being used. Normally the drivers are good about doing whatever is needed to help the individual with anything they might need until someone returns home.

For me elementary school went really well. I had great teachers; they were all very understanding and supportive of me. At that age the kids weren't mistreating me, it was more curiosity not much negativity. I didn't get asked a lot of questions. I was treated as one of them for the most part. Most kids were just happy to have another friend. I had a lot of friends that allowed me to be a part of things they were doing, whether it was a project or something in gym class. At lunch time I had people I could sit and talk to. I felt comfortable around my peers. I felt like I belonged with them.

Junior high was a little rougher, because for those two years I did not use my wheelchair at all. I was still able to walk pretty well back then. Using my crutches when rained or snowed I had to deal with wet floors as well which was very difficult but I did my best. In 7th grade I had gotten back surgery for tethered cord that caused me to lose all bowel control. I was dealing with accidents daily and having to try to hide it from my peers so I didn't get made fun of. I remember having to sit in the nurse's office waiting for someone to bring me clothes because of an accident. These were the years I did have a little more trouble with my peers. It wasn't so much being bullied but the little comments that were hurtful. I still had friends that I hung out with and that would help me. I was still able to be involved with things so I didn't feel as left out.

In high school it was even rougher than years prior. I was dealing with an even bigger school than junior high and a lot more kids. I didn't see a lot of the kids that I had grown up with and it seemed like even when I did they had changed so much. I just didn't feel like I belonged with them anymore. I struggled emotionally through high school. I never told anyone much which made things harder. I kept to myself and stayed quiet about how I was feeling. The only person that really knew anything was my cousin, Brittany, who was two years below me in school. I remember one day in my junior year of high school. which was her freshman year, I told her that someone was not treating me well. She went to that person's class and asked to talk to them. I wasn't sure what she was going to do but she stood up to them for me and told them that the way they were treating me was not acceptable and they needed to stop. For the rest of that year and the years after she would make sure she got out of classes early so that she could take me to and from my classes so nothing else would happen. It felt good having someone I could count on in the same school. It made me feel not so alone. It was even better to me because it was family and someone who already knew me and what I was capable of. I didn't feel the need to try to show her what I was able to do because she already knew and accepted things for what they were.

Chapter Seventeen

"The Ability to be involved in Activities"

Being able to be involved in activities that everyone else is doing is something very important to someone with a disability. We all want to feel included, like they're a part of the group. There are so many things that we are still able to do that would actually surprise many. We are able to go to the beach, we are able to go to parks, and be involved with school activities. It just may take a little extra time, assistance and creativity.

When I was younger I would go to the beach every year with family. I loved being in the sand, sitting by the water and even going out into the ocean. I never had a fear because I knew I was with people that would protect me. I loved sitting there watching the waves come crashing in while I dug in the sand for crabs and looking for pretty shells.

When I was smaller carrying me down to the beach wasn't a big problem but as I got older I got heavier and just wanted something a little more appropriate. We tried a regular wheelchair that did not work because the tires just sank into the sand and would get stuck. We have also tried a sled; it worked for a while because it would just glide over the sand with ease.

After trying the wheelchair and sled I had a special chair that my family had made for me that was able to get me down to the beach a lot easier. It was made of PVC pipes and had big rubber tires that would just glide over the sand. I had first discovered the chair when I was at the beach a few years prior and a couple came up to us to tell us about a chair that someone in their family had used and loved it. They told us how it was easy to get to and from the house or hotel and also were able to be taken down by the water as long as it wasn't too far in. We were able to rent one from a company associated with the beach we were at for a set price for the week. Every day when we were done with it we had to take it back and go through the rental process again in the morning. So having my own made it a lot easier and a lot more cost effective than trying to rent one.

Being in the water was one of my favorite things about the beach. I would wear a life jacket since I can't swim and always had someone with me. With my life jacket I felt free I was able to swim with whoever I was with. They were able to keep a hold of me by the straps of the life jacket without holding me back from doing what I wanted to do. I loved going through the waves just as they were about to break. The rush I would get from being in the water and seeing this wave coming at me wondering if it was going to break right on me or not is incredible.

Many people including family did not think the ocean was safe for me and they were probably right, but I was never alone. I always had at least 2 people with me. I knew that I would always be safe because the people I was with would never let anything bad happen to me.

Prior to using the life jacket I would wear arm floats but I didn't really care for those much because they would hurt my arms. I didn't like having the constriction of the arm float and having it hit my face every time I wanted to move. I also felt like as I got older and heavier they didn't hold me up as well as the life jacket does. Not having use of my legs, it was important for me to have something that would support my weight because I was only using my arms to keep me afloat.

Amusement parks were another thing I loved to do as a kid. Because of having my wheelchair I was always able to get special privileges like going to the front of the line and getting to ride twice without getting off and back in line. I was able to go on roller coasters as I got older and so many other things. A lot of people and even some family didn't think I should be riding these things and I understand their concern but it's important as an individual to stand up for yourself. We know our body and our limitations. We know what will be okay for us and what won't.

A lot of individuals need to be careful when doing things like this because it could cause more injury to their back. If you have severe back problems you should not ride these. Also anyone with a shunt should be careful not to hit their head while riding. A lot of rides toss the rider around so for someone with poor upper body strength these kinds of things may not be for them. Also having someone with the individual is important. It is helpful to have someone who can help the individual get on and off things because the people running them are not allowed to assist. So making sure we have the proper people with us is really important.

When my siblings were kids my brother was always my ride buddy. He loved any ride we could get on. We were always able to ride twice which I think made it more fun for him. He always made sure I had a good time! I'm thankful I had him because my mom and sister weren't really into all the rides that we went on. I also had the chance to go to parks with other family members as well. I loved doing things like that because I always felt like I was just like everyone else. I didn't see myself as being any different from them.

When we're at these places we need to make sure we have fun! Let ourselves go, don't hold back. This is our chance to fit in with everyone else! We shouldn't be afraid to try new things but also be aware of our limits. It's not every day we get to experience these things. Take advantage of it!

In elementary school we would go on field trips. This was always something I looked forward to. It was something I was able to do with my classmates and feel like I was one of them. I had a lot of support from my teachers, aides as well as my classmates. They all made it possible for me to be able to attend every school event I wanted to. I remember bus rides to different places sitting on the bus with my peers having fun talking and being silly. These are the moments I remember most because I felt accepted. I felt like I belonged.

In junior high I would attend all the school dances. These were fun because I would get out of the house since they were usually a Friday night after school and I would get to be with my friends. We always had a good time singing along to the music and dancing. I remember wanting to get pictures with certain people, usually boys I liked, and making my friends ask for me because I was too afraid to myself.

In high school I didn't attend many events. I kept more to myself. I did have a few people I would talk to but for the most part I did my own thing. Most of the people I grew up with had changed so much that we didn't have the same interests anymore. Everyone had their own social group in high school it was hard to find one that I fit into. I was always on the quiet side and I am even still that way now. Depending who I'm around I could be more outgoing but for the most part I'm quiet and laid back.

I would say the best part of high school for me was my senior prom. I remember not being really sure if I even wanted to go then two weeks before prom I was told I needed to have back surgery. I was upset because I thought "well there goes my chance of going even if I wanted to." I came home from the hospital with a few days to spare before prom and I said to my mom "whether I go to prom or not I'm going to be in pain so I might as well go and enjoy myself." She helped me find a dress and get it altered and I was on my way. I got there and all of my friends were surprised and happy that I made it. I'll never forget one of the most popular guys in school said to me "Oh my God sweetheart you look beautiful." It was one of the nicest things I'd heard from a classmate in a long time. That night turned into one of the best nights of my life and I'm happy that I didn't miss it.

Chapter Eighteen
"Learning How to Drive"

Learning how to drive can be very stressful for anyone but it is especially stressful for someone with a disability. This is because of how much more goes into the process for them. They have to think about a vehicle that will be efficient for them, modifications, training and so much more. In the long run though it is worth it because of the independence and freedom that comes with it!

Talking to organizations like OVR can be helpful in the process of getting a car and all the necessary modifications that go along with it. When dealing with OVR, usually the cost of the vehicle is the client's personal expense. They will fund the training if the client chooses to take it and the adaptations. If they choose not to take the training they can go through a regular DMV instead. However, if they choose to go through the classes on their own without OVR they are very expensive.

After deciding to drive of course there's the choice a vehicle! When looking for a vehicle making sure it's one that the individual can get in and out of easily, safely and independently is important. Once a vehicle is found, the next step would be setting up a payment plan. Making sure the individual can afford to pay for the car is important but can be very stressful. Asking for help with planning may be a good idea. It's a good idea to sit down and write down all of the monthly expenses to get a better idea of what the budget would be for the payments.

Now for the fun part…buying the car! Some dealerships depending on the car will actually give the buyer so much back for being disabled toward the price of the car. Now that the car is purchased arrangements for getting modifications done to it can be made. Whether they need hand controls or a lift for their chair working with the right company will make a big difference for the individual and family. Talking to friends that have had it done to their car may be good to get some ideas from them. There is no rush to making these decisions! Take your time because these are decisions that will have to be lived with and only the driver can make these choices. The driver needs to do what's comfortable and efficient for them!

My friend Brian has been showing me a lot with driving. He has been telling me what has worked and not worked for him hoping to give me ideas when I decide I want to take the leap to start driving myself. Watching him does give me confidence that one day I will be able to do it too. He takes the time to explain things to me and it really helps a lot. I don't feel strange asking him things. He's open about what you should and shouldn't do. He always tells me "no question is a stupid question." And he's right…if you're unsure of something all you have to do is ask. If you don't ask you'll never know the answer.

Even though someone may think they've done everything possible to prepare for learning to drive it is normal to still feel fear. Fear of the unknown, it's a big step to take in life and should be thought through very thoroughly. Driving is not something that should be taken lightly and may not be for everyone. That's okay! If someone doesn't feel ready to drive then they shouldn't feel pressured to do so. They need to be in control of themselves and the vehicle at all times. If that's not something they feel they can do maybe driving isn't for them. Don't feel pressured because friends are doing it or because family thinks it's the right choice. Things need to happen at the individuals own pace. I feel like people should at least try to do it but if they don't feel comfortable there's nothing that says they have to do it. There are other options.

There is a sense of freedom and independence that comes along with driving. Being able to go wherever the individual wants whenever they want is a big reason I think most young people want to drive in the first place. I think it would also give a feeling of accomplishment knowing that they did this and now they have more responsibility. Maybe people doubted them; maybe they told them that they'd never be able to drive, this is their chance to say "yes I can." And to show people what they're truly capable of doing.

Chapter Nineteen

"Entering Adulthood with a Disability"

Living in a world not meant for a person with a disability as a child is tough but imagine life as an adult. All of the responsibilities are now on us, all of the decisions...nobody there to make them for us. It can be scary for anyone but I feel like someone with a disability it's especially scary because now we're left to fend for ourselves. Maybe we've lived with our parents our whole lives; it's not an easy adjustment. It takes a lot of time, patience and support to make the adjustment into a world that was not built for someone with a disability.

Finding a house or apartment that's adapted for us is not easy. We need to make sure it has wheelchair access; making sure that the doors are wide enough, countertops are at our level and so much more. Sometimes these adaptations need to be done before the individual moves in but there are also places that offer handicap living spaces already modified. We have to do our research before making the decision to move. Being sure to visit the places to make sure they work for us and our needs. If something isn't right tell the salesperson. There may be accommodations that can be made for us and if not maybe that place isn't the one for us. Be patient there's no rush. So many people jump into the first option they see because they're in a hurry to move but later find out it doesn't work for them. Don't make this mistake. We need to take our time.

Making sure the place we move into is within our budget, making sure to talk about rent, utilities anything that we'd be responsible for. These are all things to take into consideration when looking for places to live. We need to make sure it's affordable for us to live comfortably because don't forget we're now responsible for our own meals too. And we now have to furnish our new home unless we're lucky enough to find one that is already furnished.

We have to take into consideration the distance from our new place to our family. Understandably we may want to get away and be on our own but sometimes we just need our family. It makes a big difference being 30 minutes away compared to being 10 minutes away. What if we need someone quickly? What if something goes wrong and we can't fix it ourselves? These are some things we need to ask ourselves before making the decision on our home.

Other things we should think about before moving out on our own is a job…how are we going to afford our home? Transportation…we need to get to and from our job to pay for our home. Finances…we now need to budget our money so we have what we need for our new home, as well as food, clothes, gas for our car, and any other necessities. Being an adult is not easy especially being an adult with a disability but if we put your mind to it and work hard we can achieve anything!

Now that we're on our own, we need to be more responsible with all of our doctor's appointments and other appointments we may need to get to. Making sure we have the proper ways to get to and from these appointments, making sure we set alarms for ourselves and reminders is important. This is all part of being responsible in adulthood.

Someone may say "well, what about my friends?" Friends may be able to do some things but remember they have lives too. Maybe they have their own families now to take care of they're not always going to be able to drop everything. This is why being responsible is so important! Nobody ever said adulthood was going to be easy but it is worth it! When it comes down to having to do something ourselves we are a lot stronger than we think! Don't give up!

Chapter Twenty

"The Struggles of College and Finding a Job"

Finding a job is never easy for anyone, but having a disability makes it even harder. We have to look for jobs we are capable of and that we have the degree for. If the individual has gone to college for a specific career finding things we can specialize in while still doing what we love is important. We can't settle for anything less than what will make us happy.

Once the individual finds and starts their job fitting in with their environment could be difficult. What I did when I started working was told my bosses first thing what my problems were, what may or may not happen, what I may or may not need and it worked out well for me. My supervisors are supportive of me and have done a lot over the years to accommodate me and my needs. Being open and not hiding anything has been the best for me. I feel like they respected me even more for my honesty. And it shows that I am taking things seriously.

Getting along with coworkers plays a big part because the individual will need to be able to tolerate them every day. I'm not saying we have to be best friends but being able to work with them smoothly and feel like they listen to personal input is important. There will be times when things happen and don't go the way we want but how we handle those situations is what's important. People will talk behind our back but as long as we keep our head up we'll make it. We can't let the negativity get us down. Being the best person we can be, doing the job to the best of our ability and ignore the haters will make things go more smoothly!

Doing our best to complete our job independently will show the supervisors that we were the right choice for the job. While doing our jobs we also have to be safe. Being sure not to do something that will cause injury to us is very important. Our bodies are not as durable as most individuals so we need to be more cautious of what we do.

Being on time for our shift and not calling off will show everyone the dedicated person that we are. Understandably everyone gets sick and things happen but we shouldn't make a habit of it. When something does happen that we need to take time off be honest with supervisors and bring documentation whenever possible as proof that what we said was really the truth.

Bringing necessary supplies with us to our job and making sure we're taken care of medically is extremely important. Accidents happen but nothing is more embarrassing than having to tell someone we had a problem and don't have anything with us. Some jobs have lockers for employees to use. Keeping extra clothes and supplies in our locker as well will help us make sure we always have something with us. It's always better to be safe than sorry.

Taking advantage of our disability is not something that would be taken lightly at most jobs. Just because we can technically get away with something doesn't mean we should always use the disability as an excuse for things. Everyone understands things happen but not making it a habit will make us look better in the eyes of others. It will show the strong individuals that we truly are.

Chapter Twenty One

"Healthy Relationships in Love"

Finding someone who truly accepts us for the person we are is sometimes difficult. Look for the person who will do anything for us just to see us happy. It doesn't matter what they look like or how much they have to offer physically, it's what is on the inside that counts the most. We should look for someone who doesn't see our disability. Someone who sees the person inside, the loving, caring person we are.

Someone who has compassion will make a good companion because they want to see us happy. They will want to do what's best for us. They're the type of person that would go out of their way just to make sure we had what we needed.

The right person would be understanding of us and our needs. They would understand that things happen and sometimes we can't control it. This type of person would never get angry at us for things out of our control instead they would be right by our side helping us through it. They would be supportive and encouraging of us. Having a person who truly cares would not leave us to clean up our mess alone. Instead they would be right beside us working with us.

Finding a person like this can be difficult but if we are patient we'll find that person. We should never settle for anything less than we deserve. Going out with our friends, being open to trying new things and the right person will find us. There's no need to go looking for "our person." They will find us when the time is right. It's all about timing when it comes to relationships and love. There is no rush to finding the person. It takes a lot of time, patience and perseverance.

When we find that special someone, it's important to take our time. Not rushing into anything until we know it's what both want and what will make you both happy. Making sure they know everything they might need to know about us before things get too serious. I wouldn't tell them everything all at once or too soon into the relationship but at the same time I wouldn't wait too long. It's all about timing. When we feel we're comfortable and ready that's when that conversation should happen. If the individual doesn't feel they can, if they feel like their partner won't understand maybe they should think about is this person truly right for them. If they have the right person they should be able to tell them anything right? Taking baby steps telling them what they need to know first will help ease the nervousness a little bit. If the individual gives a good reaction then maybe next time it can be taken a little further.

The person we're going to be with for life should essentially know us inside and out, good and bad. If they can't stick around for the ups and downs they aren't the one for us. Next to our family this person should be the one that is able to take care of us when we need it the most. We often take for granted being able to do things for ourselves but what if something happens and our spouse needs to do this for us? Then what? We need to feel comfortable and confident enough to let this person take care of us. We have to feel like they're capable and that we'll be okay!

The biggest part of being with someone is marriage and family. For most of us this is a big dream. Let's face it, who doesn't want to get all dressed up for the big day and have fun with family and friends?! Just be sure that this is the person to spend the rest of our life with.

Chapter Twenty Two
"Starting a Family"

Having a family is something very important to a lot of people, especially women. Even people with disabilities dream of having a family with children. Whether it's having their own child or through a surrogate or even adoption many people will do anything to have a child. There are so many babies that are given up for adoption waiting to go into loving homes. People who struggle to conceive are the perfect people for these children.

If someone with a disability decides to try ourselves regular visits to our doctor is important to make sure that we are healthy enough to have a baby of our own. This is when we will also find out if we're actually able to conceive. Some women with spina bifida are unable to conceive a child due to infertility. At the doctor they will run blood tests just to make sure we're in good health medically to carry a child. They will look for underlying problems that maybe we didn't even know we had. At this appointment they may even tell us about other options we may have such as adoption or a surrogate.

Through the pregnancy we will need to be checked regularly for our health, as well as the baby. The doctors will perform regular ultrasounds to check on the baby, listen to the heartbeat and look for any abnormalities that may occur. If you or your spouse have spina bifida there is a higher chance of the baby having it as well. And sometimes even if neither of the parents have it they can still have a baby who does. It doesn't mean they've done anything wrong. Taking folic acid will help to possibly lessen the chances of this happening but there is still that chance.

If they choose to go through with a surrogate then another woman would carry the baby. The doctor would implant the females eggs with the spouse's sperm into the surrogate's uterus and if fertilized she would become pregnant and carry the baby for the couple. I know it's not the same as being pregnant and females want that experience but she needs to think about what's going to be most healthy for her and the life she's bringing into the world.

Once the couple brings that baby home, their life is going to be a lot different. In a good way of course! They get to raise that little life they made and take care of it the way their mom took care of them when they were babies. Having support from spouses, family and friends will be the most important part of raising the child. Knowing that they are there to count on to help will make anyone be a better parent.

The couple will have to get used to being up at night when the baby doesn't sleep, changing diapers, bottle feeds, and so much more. You and your spouse will have to figure out who will do what and what times. It's going to take a lot of teamwork from both of you.

Once the child gets old enough the decision will have to be made whether going back to work or being a stay at home parent is best for the family. This decision will be hard but you have to think of expenses. Can you afford daycare or a babysitter? If the answer is yes, then give it a try. There's no harm in trying! It's better to try and realize it can't be done than to not try and wonder. That goes for anything in life. We need to try different things. Push ourselves as much as we can because if we don't we'll always stay in the same place.

Acknowledgements

I want to thank my family for all the love and support you've shown me my whole life! I would not be the person I am today if it weren't for you! Through everything I've gone through you have been my rock. I always knew I could lean on all of you for anything! Good times and bad we have stuck together and pushed through. I couldn't have done it without each and every one of you!

Mom, I can't thank you enough for shaping me into the woman I am today. I wouldn't be where I am if I didn't have you standing beside me. You have been there for me through everything good and bad. There aren't enough words or paper to say how I feel. You have always shown me love and compassion, sometimes tough love too. I am a better person because of you. You have inspired me to be the strong woman I am today. Everything you have dealt with and yet you continue to push through is inspiring!

Alexis, at 7 ½ years old I was blessed with the best gift a girl could ask for! A sister! You have been my best friend from the time you were a baby! The bond we share is something I could never replace. You have supported me through so much and continue to do so still! You have taught me that it's okay to be silly and come out of your shell. You have shown me nothing but love and compassion. Even as a little girl helping me with wounds and anything else I may have needed. You never turned away. I can't express how much that means to me. You have defended me when it was needed and have put me in my place too but I know it's only because you love me.

Aaron, I am grateful to have a brother like you! You sometimes show me tough love but I know it is love all the same. You've helped me through so much and have defended me when you felt the need. I can't thank you enough! Though you drive me crazy and torment me I know it's only out of love. I still remember the day you called me about the hand bike you found online. I was sick and not feeling like going anywhere but I got up and went anyway. You sounded so proud of what you found. It made me feel good knowing you thought of me. I appreciate you always looking out for me! It means a lot! It's been amazing having a brother like you! I can't imagine my life without you!

Julian, at 3 years old you have taught me so much. You are one of the smartest little boys I know! Though you may not understand, I want to thank you for always being the little push I needed to get things done. I love how you don't see me as someone with a disability, you see me as someone who will play with you and have fun. That means the world to me! One day you will grow up into a loving and caring young man. Tillie loves you Juju!

Caitlin, bestie where do I even begin?! 18 years of being best friends, you've seen me at my worst and at my best. You have picked me up when I was down. You've always shown me that I could trust you with anything and that nothing could ever come between us! I can't tell you how thankful I am to have found a friend like you! You are definitely like a sister to me. We have a bond that I can't get with anyone else. We understand each other like nobody else would believe. We have helped each other through so much and I'm so grateful to have you by my side. I don't know what I'd do without you and I hope to never find out!

Brian, you have been one of my best friends from the time I was 19 years old. We have been through so much together. You've taught me a lot about life on your own and I'm grateful for that. Anytime I have a question about something you're more than willing to show me. You're crazy but so am I so it's okay! You have shown me that anything is possible with teamwork. I never thought we'd be able to go out alone together with 2 chairs and neither of us able to stand but we did! We have accomplished so much on our own and I'm proud to say you're my friend! I know we've had our tough times but we pushed through them together and I feel like that made our friendship stronger. I don't know where I'd be without you!

Thank you everyone who has made this book possible and that has supported me through it all! I don't know what I would do without my amazing family and friends! Everyone that I didn't personally mention just know that what you do does not go unnoticed! I am grateful for all of my family and friends for everything you do!

Thank you!

Made in the USA
Middletown, DE
15 November 2019